2 2 MAY 2018

The Queen, the Mice and the Cheese

A humorous
fantasy story

30130 162658909

First published in 2006 by
Franklin Watts
338 Euston Road
London
NW1 3BH

Franklin Watts Australia
Hachette Children's Books
Level 17/207 Kent Street
Sydney
NSW 2000

Text © Carrie Weston 2006
Illustration © Martin Remphry 2006

The rights of Carrie Weston to be identified as the
author and Martin Remphry as the illustrator of this Work
have been asserted in accordance with the Copyright,
Designs and Patents Act, 1988.

All rights reserved. No part of this publication may be
reproduced, stored in a retrieval system, or transmitted
in any form or by any means, electronic, mechanical,
photocopy, recording or otherwise, without the prior
written permission of the copyright owner.

A CIP catalogue record for this book is available
from the British Library.

ISBN 0 7496 6563 7 (hbk)
ISBN 0 7496 6566 1 (pbk)

Series Editor: Jackie Hamley
Series Advisors: Dr Barrie Wade, Dr Hilary Minns
Design: Peter Scoulding

Printed in China

The Queen, the Mice and the Cheese

Written by
Carrie Weston

Illustrated by
Martin Remphry

W
FRANKLIN WATTS
LONDON•SYDNEY

Carrie Weston

"The Queen in this story has the answer to her problem right under her nose! Has that ever happened to you?"

Martin Remphry

"I work in a studio in 'The Old Lost Goods Building'. This is where the things people left behind on trains used to be kept, such as glasses and false teeth!"

Once there was a Queen who
lived in a splendid palace.

She loved her rich furniture ...

she loved her fine clothes ...

she loved her beautiful garden.

But most of all, the Queen
loved cheese.

The royal kitchen was full of cheese.

There was hard cheese ...

and soft cheese ...

and blue cheese.

There was even cheese with holes in.

9

It was not just the Queen who loved cheese. All the mice in the land loved cheese, too. Before long, they started to visit the palace.

Soon there were mice

in the cupboards ...

under the table ...

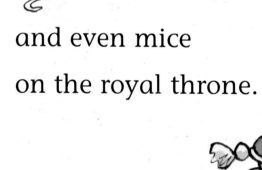

and even mice

on the royal throne.

The Queen threw up her hands in horror. She called for her ministers. "Cats!" they said, nodding wisely. "Send for some cats!"

So all the cats in the land were
invited to the palace to chase
away the mice. And they did.

When the mice were gone, the cats made themselves at home. They dozed on the royal bed ...

and sharpened their claws on the throne.

The Queen was horrified.

She called for her ministers again.

"Dogs!" they said at last. "Send for

some dogs to chase away the cats."

All the dogs in the land were invited
to the royal palace. The dogs quickly
chased away the cats.

Then the dogs made themselves at home. They chewed up the Queen's slippers.

They buried bones in the royal gardens.

"Enough!" cried the Queen in
despair. "Where are my ministers?"

19

The ministers sat around and scratched their heads. At last, they had an answer. "Elephants!" they cried. "Bring in some elephants."

Soon the palace was full of
elephants. When the dogs saw them,
they ran away as fast as they could.

The elephants loved their new home.

They squashed the sofas.

They splashed in the pond.

And they were far too big to squeeze through the doors. "Oh, my splendid palace!" yelled the Queen.

The ministers came at once.

They looked in big books.

Then they all nodded wisely.

"We have an answer!" they said.

"Mice!" announced the ministers.
"Elephants are afraid of mice!"
The ministers were very pleased
with themselves.

The Queen was not quite so pleased, but she had an idea. First, she watched as the mice chased all the elephants out of the palace.

Then the Queen called the mice
to her meeting room. The Queen
made two rules.

1. Mice may only eat Cheese labelled "Cheese for mice."

2. Mice will not bring Cats, dogs, or elephants to the Palace.

The mice chatted amongst themselves. Then they nodded and signed the Queen's rules.

When the builders had finished,
the Queen once again lived in
a splendid palace.

And she was very happy to share her cheese with the mice – just as long as they kept to the rules!

Notes for parents and teachers

READING CORNER has been structured to provide maximum support for new readers. The stories may be used by adults for sharing with young children. Primarily, however, the stories are designed for newly independent readers, whether they are reading these books in bed at night, or in the reading corner at school or in the library.

Starting to read alone can be a daunting prospect. **READING CORNER** helps by providing visual support and repeating words and phrases, while making reading enjoyable. These books will develop confidence in the new reader, and encourage a love of reading that will last a lifetime!

If you are reading this book with a child, here are a few tips:

1. Make reading fun! Choose a time to read when you and the child are relaxed and have time to share the story.

2. Encourage children to reread the story, and to retell the story in their own words, using the illustrations to remind them what has happened.

3. Give praise! Remember that small mistakes need not always be corrected.

READING CORNER covers three grades of early reading ability, with three levels at each grade. Each level has a certain number of words per story, indicated by the number of bars on the spine of the book, to allow you to choose the right book for a young reader:

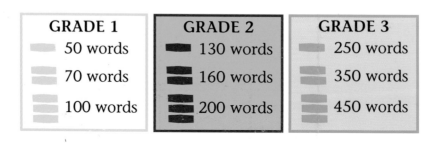

GRADE 1	GRADE 2	GRADE 3
50 words	130 words	250 words
70 words	160 words	350 words
100 words	200 words	450 words